Carlos & Carmen

Tooth Trouble

by Kirsten McDonald
illustrated by Fátima Anaya

Calico Kid
An Imprint of Magic Wagon
abdopublishing.com

For Bonnie, always ready with a pen and rainbow paper —KKM

This book is for my mom, gracias por siempre apoyarme en todo.
I love you so much. —FA

abdopublishing.com

Published by Magic Wagon, a division of ABDO, PO Box 398166, Minneapolis, Minnesota 55439.

Printed in the United States of America, North Mankato, Minnesota.
082017
012018

Written by Kirsten McDonald
Illustrated by Fátima Anaya
Edited by Heidi M.D. Elston
Design Contributors: Christina Doffing & Candice Keimig

Publisher's Cataloging-in-Publication Data

Names: McDonald, Kirsten, author. | Anaya, Fátima, illustrator.
Title: Tooth trouble / by Kirsten McDonald; illustrated by Fátima Anaya.
Description: Minneapolis, Minnesota : Magic Wagon, 2018. | Series: Carlos & Carmen
Summary: Carmen is keeping the tooth fairy busy. She's lost her two front teeth, and now one of her bottom teeth is wiggling every which way. But Carlos can't even get one tooth to wiggle, even a tiny bit. He hasn't had a single visit from the tooth fairy. Find out how Carlos and Carmen take care of Carlos's tooth trouble.
Identifiers: LCCN 2017946422 | ISBN 9781532130366 (lib.bdg.) | ISBN 9781532130960 (ebook) | ISBN 9781532131264 (Read-to-me ebook)
Subjects: LCSH: Hispanic American families--Juvenile fiction. | Imagination in children--Juvenile fiction. | Brothers and sisters--Juvenile fiction. | Teeth--Mobility--Juvenile fiction.
Classification: DDC [E]--dc23
LC record available at https://lccn.loc.gov/2017946422

Table of Contents

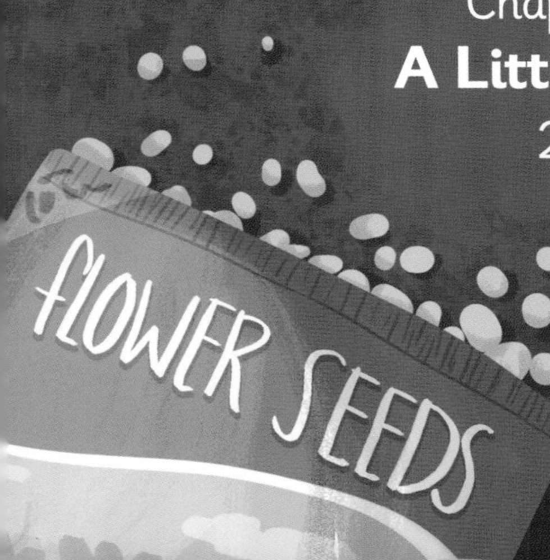

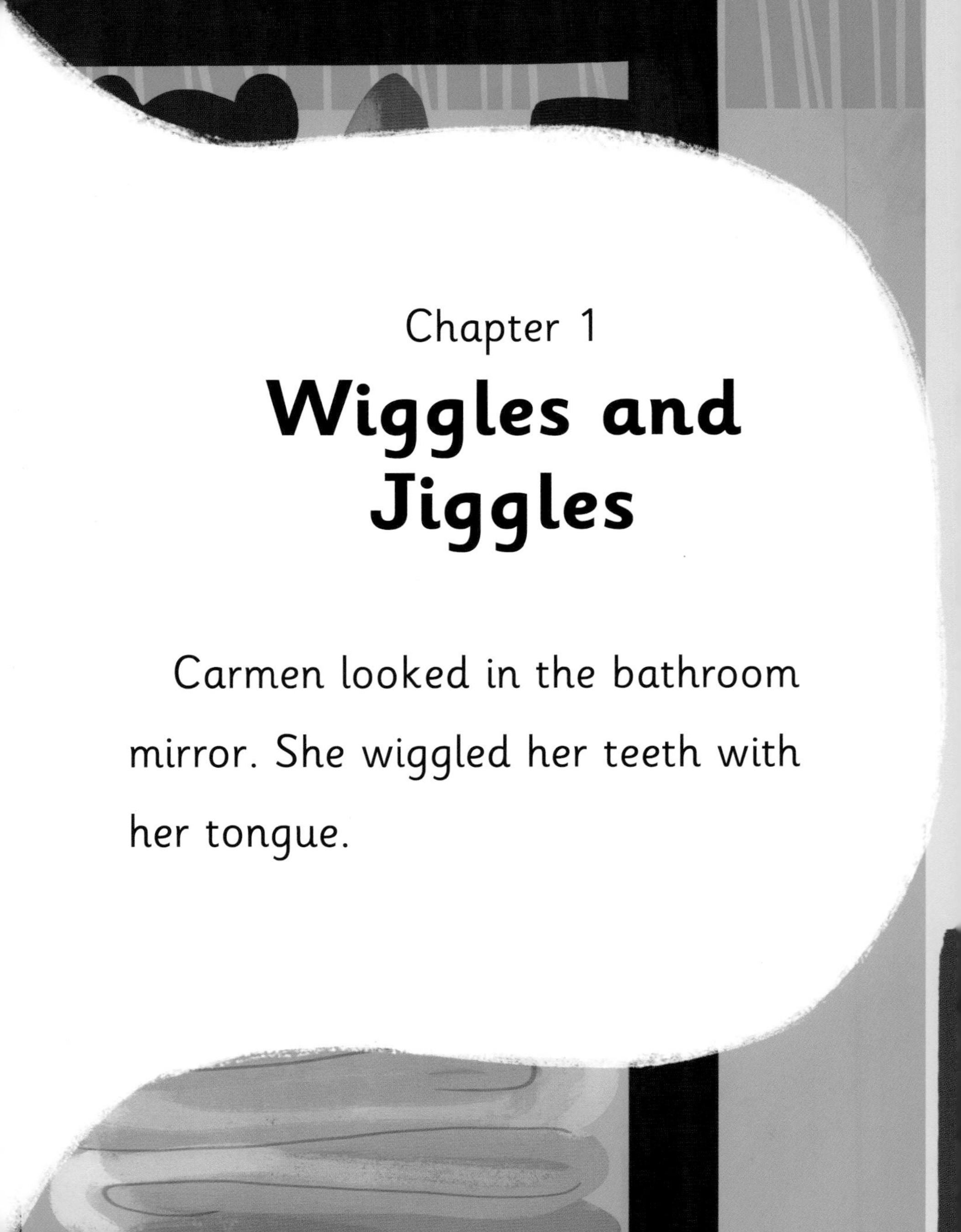

Chapter 1

Wiggles and Jiggles

Carmen looked in the bathroom mirror. She wiggled her teeth with her tongue.

“!Mira, Carlos!” she said. “Look how loose my teeth are.”

Carlos watched Carmen’s teeth wiggle. He looked at the spaces where she was already missing two teeth. Then he looked in the mirror at his own teeth.

He tried pushing on his teeth with his tongue. He tried pressing on them with his fingers. But he could not make any of his teeth wiggle.

"I still don't have a loose tooth," Carlos said sadly.

Carmen looked at her twin. "You can have my next diente that comes out," she offered.

"Will the tooth fairy come if it's not my tooth?" Carlos asked.

Carmen wiggled her teeth some more. She said, "Maybe so, since we're gemelos."

All that morning, Carmen's teeth wiggled and jiggled.

When she ran, her teeth wiggled. When she jumped, her teeth jiggled. And when she cartwheeled, her teeth wiggled and jiggled all around.

Carlos ran and jumped and rolled. His teeth did not wiggle. His teeth did not jiggle. His teeth did not move even a tiny bit.

Chapter 2
Rocks

Later that day, Carlos and Carmen were playing on their tire swing.

Carlos held the rope with one hand. With his other hand, he tested a tooth. "Not even a little wiggle."

"Try a different diente," suggested Carmen. Then she pushed the tire swing.

Carlos tried another tooth. He tried another and another and another. But no matter how hard he pushed or pulled, his teeth would not wiggle.

“¡Mis hijos!” called Mamá and Papá from the garden. “We need your help.”

The twins ran to the garden. Mamá gave them each a small shovel. “We need to get the soil ready for our garden. You can help by taking out the rocas.”

The twins dug with little shovels. Whenever they found a rock, they put it in their buckets.

"¡Mira, Carmen!" said Carlos. He held up a rock. "This roca looks like a piece of candy."

The twins dug some more.

"!Mira, Carlos!" said Carmen. She held up a rock. "This roca looks like an egg."

The twins dug some more.

Carlos held up a tiny, white rock. "And this roca looks like a tooth."

Carmen looked at Carlos. Carlos looked at Carmen. Then they both looked at the rock.

"Are you thinking what I'm thinking?" they asked at the same time. And because they were twins, they were.

Chapter 3

Pillows and Paper

That night Carlos asked, "Will this roca fool the tooth fairy?"

"Tal vez," said Carmen. "It looks like a diente to me."

"But the tooth fairy is a tooth expert," said Carlos doubtfully.

"Sí," agreed Carmen. "But it will be dark when she comes."

"And, maybe, she won't look too closely," added Carlos. He placed the little, white rock under his pillow.

"Buenas noches," he said as he snuggled under his covers.

"Buenas noches," Carmen said as she turned off her twin's light.

In the morning, Carmen raced to Carlos's room. "Did she come?" she asked.

Carlos reached under his pillow. "¡Sí!" said Carlos as he pulled out a piece of paper.

The paper was the size of a dollar. It was the shape of a dollar. But, it was not a dollar.

“It’s a picture of a dollar,” said Carlos disappointedly.

“Tal vez, the tooth fairy can see in the dark,” said Carmen.

Carmen's tongue pressed on her loose teeth. Suddenly, a tooth popped out and bounced onto the bed.

"I lost another tooth," said Carmen with surprise.

Carmen looked at her twin. She looked at the picture of the dollar.

Carmen picked up her tooth. "You can have my diente," she said. "And since we're gemelos, maybe my tooth will work for you."

"Yo no sé," said Carlos. "I think maybe it has to be your own tooth."

"Maybe," said Carmen as she slid her tooth under Carlos's pillow. "But, just in case, let's try it."

Chapter 4

A Little Help

The next morning, Carmen rushed into Carlos's room. "Did the tooth fairy come?" she asked.

Carlos reached under his pillow. Carmen's tooth was gone. In its place was a folded piece of paper.

"She left you a letter," Carmen said excitedly. "Open it up and see what it says."

Carlos read, “The tooth you leave must be your own. I know you’ll lose one before you’re grown.”

Carmen tried to make Carlos feel better. “It’s a really nice note.”

“I guess,” said Carlos. He pushed his teeth with his tongue. “But what if I never lose any teeth?”

“Let’s go see Mamá and Papá,” said Carmen. “They’ll know what to do.”

The twins ran to the kitchen. Mamá and Papá were making breakfast.

"¡Mamá! ¡Papá!" called Carmen. "We need your help!"

"¡Mis hijos!" cried Mamá. "What is the matter?"

"It's Carlos," said Carmen. "He's got tooth trouble."

Papá looked at Carmen's gap-toothed smile. He teased, "I'd say you're the one with tooth trouble, Carmencita."

"Try eating something chewy or crunchy for breakfast," said Mamá.

Mamá put a chewy bagel on Carlos's plate. Papá added a red apple.

Carlos crunched into the apple. He chomped and chewed the bagel. Then, he tried wiggling his teeth.

"Any luck?" asked Papá.

"Not yet," said Carlos.

"Try wiggling your dientes with this tissue," said Carmen.

Carlos wrapped the tissue around one of his teeth. He pushed and pulled the tooth. Carlos's eyes got big. "I think I felt a wiggle," he said.

"Let me try," said Carmen. She gave the tooth a push and a pull. "It's definitely loose."

"Hooray!" shouted Mamá.

"Double hooray!" shouted Carlos.

Papá laughed. He hugged the twins and said, "Now you both have tooth trouble."

Spanish to English

buenas noches – good night

diente – tooth

gemelos – twins

Mamá – Mommy

¡Mira! – Look!

mis hijos – my children

Papá – Daddy

roca – rock

sí – yes

tal vez – maybe

Yo no sé – I don't know